For my mother with love – R.K.
For Giulio with love – T.M.

VIKING
Published by the Penguin Group
Viking Penguin, a division of Penguin Books USA Inc.,
375 Hudson Street, New York, New York 10014, U.S.A.
Penguin Books Ltd, 27 Wrights Lane, London W8 5TZ, England
Penguin Books Ltd, Ringwood, Victoria, Australia
Penguin Books Canada Ltd, 2801 John Street, Markham, Ontario, Canada L3R 1B4
Penguin Books (N.Z.) Ltd, 182–190 Wairau Road, Auckland 10, New Zealand

Penguin Books Ltd, Registared Offices: Harmondsworth, Middlesex, England

First published in South Africa by Songololo Books 1989
First American edition published 1991

1 3 5 7 9 10 8 6 4 2

Text copyright © Rosemary Kahn, 1989
Illustrations copyright © Terry Milne, 1989
All rights reserved

Library of Congress catalog Card Number: 90-50986
ISBN 0-670-84023-8

Printed and bound in Hong Kong
by Dai Nippon Printing Co. (H. K.) Ltd.

GRANDMA'S HAT

Written by Rosemary Kahn

Illustrated by Terry Milne

VIKING

"Please tell us the story of your hat, Grandma!"
said Sally, flopping down on the floor beside
her grandmother's chair.

"Yes, please," said Nancy and Nicola together.

Andrew climbed on to Grandma's lap. He
loved to hear her stories.

"Oh, *that* funny story," said Grandma.

She settled back in her chair and closed her
eyes for a moment, as if remembering some
far-off time.

"Once upon a time..." Grandma began.

"Once upon a time?" echoed Nicola. "Is this a fairy tale?"

"No, dear," said Grandma, "it's a true story, but it happened a long time ago and all old stories begin with 'once upon a time'." She began again.

"Once upon a time, when I was about your age, Sally, I lived with my parents and my two younger sisters, Gabrielle and Joy, in a small town called De Aar, in the Karoo. In summer it was so hot and dusty that water was more precious than gold.

"My father, your great-grandpa, was a shopkeeper. He had the biggest and the best shop in the town. My mother used to help him in the shop in the mornings. When we were old enough we were allowed to help in the shop, too.

"I loved the smell of that shop. My father
sold most things, from soap to sugar. From
clothes to tablecloths. Shops in those days
were different from the ones you know.

"The shopkeepers stood behind long counters
and brought everything the customers wanted.
My father knew all his regular customers by name,
and always had time for a chat.

"He certainly loved his work but his pride and joy was his motorcar. It was called a Hupmobile.

"It had a folding roof and sides that could be taken off. It also had very comfortable soft leather seats. We all thought it was the grandest car in the world.

"On Sundays, we would put on our best clothes and my father would take us for a drive. Sometimes, we just drove into the country, but most often we went visiting.

"The Karoo is sheep-farming country and many of our friends lived on big sheep-farms.

"Now, Sunday-best clothes, in those days, included hats. None of us complained about our hats, until one year my mother bought me the ugliest hat I had ever seen!

"It was a horrible yellowy-mustard color, which she called 'old gold.' I hated it. It looked just like a potty turned upside down – without the handle, of course!

"My sisters laughed and invented rude names for it. And when my best friend Elise saw it she laughed so much that tears ran down her cheeks! I wanted to cry, but I didn't. I was too proud.

"One fine Sunday morning," Grandma
continued, "when my father had washed and
polished the car and we were all decked out
in our Sunday-best, we set off on a long drive
to visit the Marais family. They lived on a very
big sheep-farm and we loved going there.
There were often baby lambs, and they had
cats and dogs and horses as well.

"Well, the road to the farm was very flat. There was nothing much to see along the way, besides some clumps of grass and the odd thorn bush. To pass the time, we sang.

"So there we were, driving along and singing away merrily, when all of a sudden a little breeze sprang up. I tilted my head back just a little, and suddenly I didn't have an ugly mustard-colored hat anymore! I didn't even look back to see where it had landed. I just went on singing as if nothing had happened.

"When we arrived at the farmhouse,
Gabrielle noticed that the hat was missing.
'Look, look, Stell's hat has gone!' she cried.
Everyone stared at me. 'It was the wind,'
I muttered...

"Mama said, 'Oh, Estelle, your new hat...'
and she looked quite sad, but she said nothing
more, because just at that moment our friends
appeared, and so, for a while, I was safe.

"By the time we left, it was late. My mother kept on giving me those 'I'm-not-very-pleased-with-you' looks but she didn't say a word. I almost wished she would scold me and have it over with.

"There was no singing on the way home and my father had put up the hood of the car, as the air was quite cold. My two sisters slept, but I sat as rigid as a poker between them, waiting for my punishment.

"When we arrived home, Papa put his arm around me and gave me a hug. I knew that he understood about that hat.

"In the end all Mama said was that I would
have no spending money for a month as she
would have to save it for a new hat.

"Well, before the month was up, Papa came back from a visit to Kimberley, which was a much bigger town than ours, and he brought with him a new hat for me.

"It was the color of soft green moss in springtime. I thought it was the most beautiful hat I had ever seen and I have never enjoyed wearing any other hat as much as I did that one.

"A few weeks later, we went to visit the Van der Heevers. We set off in the same direction as before and we sang all the way. I was singing loudly, because I was so happy with my new hat, and I almost missed seeing the scarecrow. He was dressed in sacking trousers and an old check shirt and on his head was my awful hat. A little dusty and worse for wear, but very definitely my mustard-colored potty hat!

"Papa said that the scarecrow needed it far more than I did! He warned us not to tell the Van der Heevers that the hat the scarecrow was wearing belonged to me. He didn't want to embarrass them.

"But during lunch Mr Van der Heever said to Papa, 'Dan, what do you think of the scarecrow in my vegetable field?' The Van der Heevers must have wondered why my sisters and I started giggling when Papa replied, 'Anton, I've never seen such a fine scarecrow – no bird would dare come near that dreadful hat!'"